SALINA FREE LIBRARY
100 BELMONT STREET
MATTYDALE, NY 13211

Extreme Sports

PARKOUR

Lily Loye

DiscoverRoo
An Imprint of Pop!
popbooksonline.com

abdobooks.com

Published by Pop!, a division of ABDO, PO Box 398166, Minneapolis, Minnesota 55439. Copyright © 2021 by POP, LLC. International copyrights reserved in all countries. No part of this book may be reproduced in any form without written permission from the publisher. Pop!™ is a trademark and logo of POP, LLC.

Printed in the United States of America, North Mankato, Minnesota.

052020
092020

THIS BOOK CONTAINS RECYCLED MATERIALS

Cover Photo: iStockphoto
Interior Photos: iStockphoto, 1, 6, 7, 8, 9, 22, 23, 27, 28, 29, 30, 31; Shutterstock Images, 5, 11, 18–19; Henny Ray Abrams/AP Images, 12; Sipa Asia/Sipa USA/Newscom, 13; Yang Xiaoyuan/Xinhua News Agency/Newscom, 14; M.G.M./Allnut, Susan/Album/Newscom, 15; Amr Abdallah Dalsh/Reuters/Newscom, 17; Kenjiro Matsuo/Aflo Sport/Newscom, 20, 21; Javier Lira Otero/Notimex/Newscom, 25

Editor: Brienna Rossiter
Series Designer: Jake Slavik

Library of Congress Control Number: 2019954960
Publisher's Cataloging-in-Publication Data
Names: Loye, Lily, author.
Title: Parkour / by Lily Loye
Description: Minneapolis, Minnesota : POP!, 2021 | Series: Extreme sports | Includes online resources and index.
Identifiers: ISBN 9781532167836 (lib. bdg.) | ISBN 9781532168932 (ebook)
Subjects: LCSH: Parkour--Juvenile literature. | PK (Parkour)--Juvenile literature. | Extreme sports--Juvenile literature. | Sports--Juvenile literature.
Classification: DDC 796.046--dc23

WELCOME TO DiscoverRoo!

Pop open this book and you'll find QR codes loaded with information, so you can learn even more!

Scan this code* and others like it while you read, or visit the website below to make this book pop!

popbooksonline.com/parkour

*Scanning QR codes requires a web-enabled smart device with a QR code reader app and a camera.

TABLE OF CONTENTS

CHAPTER 1
What Is Parkour? 4

CHAPTER 2
History 10

CHAPTER 3
Parkour Today 16

CHAPTER 4
Safety 26

Making Connections 30
Glossary 31
Index 32
Online Resources 32

Chapter 1
What is Parkour?

A man runs to the end of an alley. A tall wall blocks his way. But at the last second, the man jumps. He seems to walk up the wall. Then he grabs a small ledge. He pulls himself up onto the roof.

Watch a video here!

Climbing a wall requires strong muscles.

When practicing parkour, people often make huge leaps.

The man sprints to the roof's edge. Then he jumps. He leaps 6 feet (1.8 m) and lands on the next building. It is a parking garage. The man runs to a set of stairs. He **vaults** over the railing. He does a series of flips to reach the bottom. Then he runs down the sidewalk.

Vaults are moves that help people move quickly past obstacles.

Any part of a city can become an obstacle for parkour.

The man is practicing parkour. He uses the city as an **obstacle course**.

He tries to find the fastest route through it. People who do parkour are called **traceurs**. They jump, run, and climb. They may even do tricks along the way.

Parkour is about moving creatively. Traceurs often follow unusual paths.

DID YOU KNOW? When people get together to practice parkour, it's called a jam.

CHAPTER 2
HISTORY

Parkour got its start in France in the 1980s. It was based on **obstacle course** training. Raymond Belle learned about this kind of training in the French military. He taught it to his son, David.

LEARN MORE HERE!

Athletes and soldiers use obstacle courses to stay strong.

David Belle founded parkour with a group of eight friends.

David Belle and his friends practiced in their hometown of Lisses, France. They treated the city like an obstacle course.

They ran and jumped through streets and buildings. The friends made videos showing their moves.

Traceurs jump and climb on rooftops.

DID YOU KNOW? The name *parkour* comes from the French word *parcours*. It means "path" or "course."

At some parkour events, people move through courses set up to resemble cities.

People in other countries took notice. More and more people began to practice parkour. By 2009, MTV had a show called

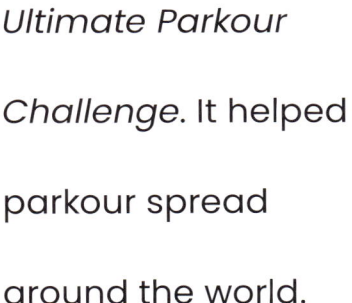

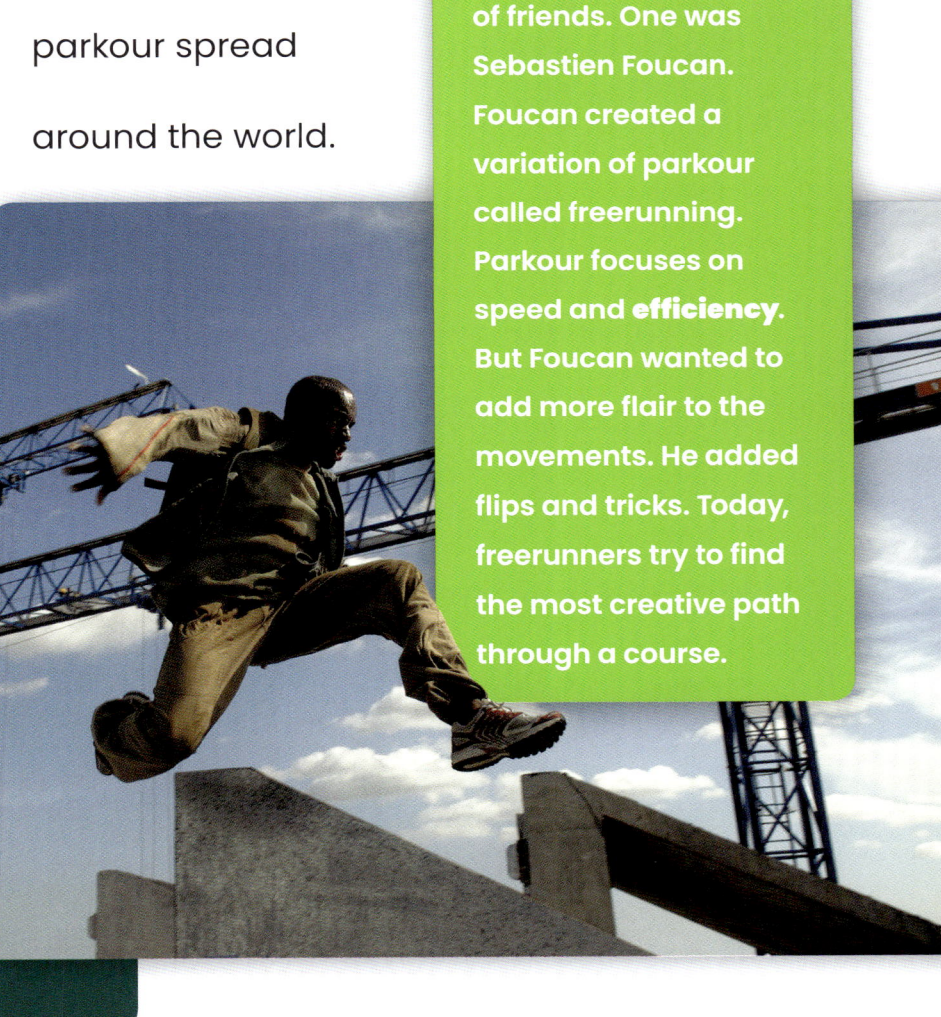

Ultimate Parkour Challenge. It helped parkour spread around the world.

FREERUNNING

David Belle practiced parkour with a group of friends. One was Sebastien Foucan. Foucan created a variation of parkour called freerunning. Parkour focuses on speed and **efficiency**. But Foucan wanted to add more flair to the movements. He added flips and tricks. Today, freerunners try to find the most creative path through a course.

CHAPTER 3
PARKOUR TODAY

Parkour did not start as a competitive sport. Instead, **traceurs** practiced with friends. Each person focused on building skills and strength. Some traceurs still do this. They don't believe in competing.

COMPLETE AN ACTIVITY HERE!

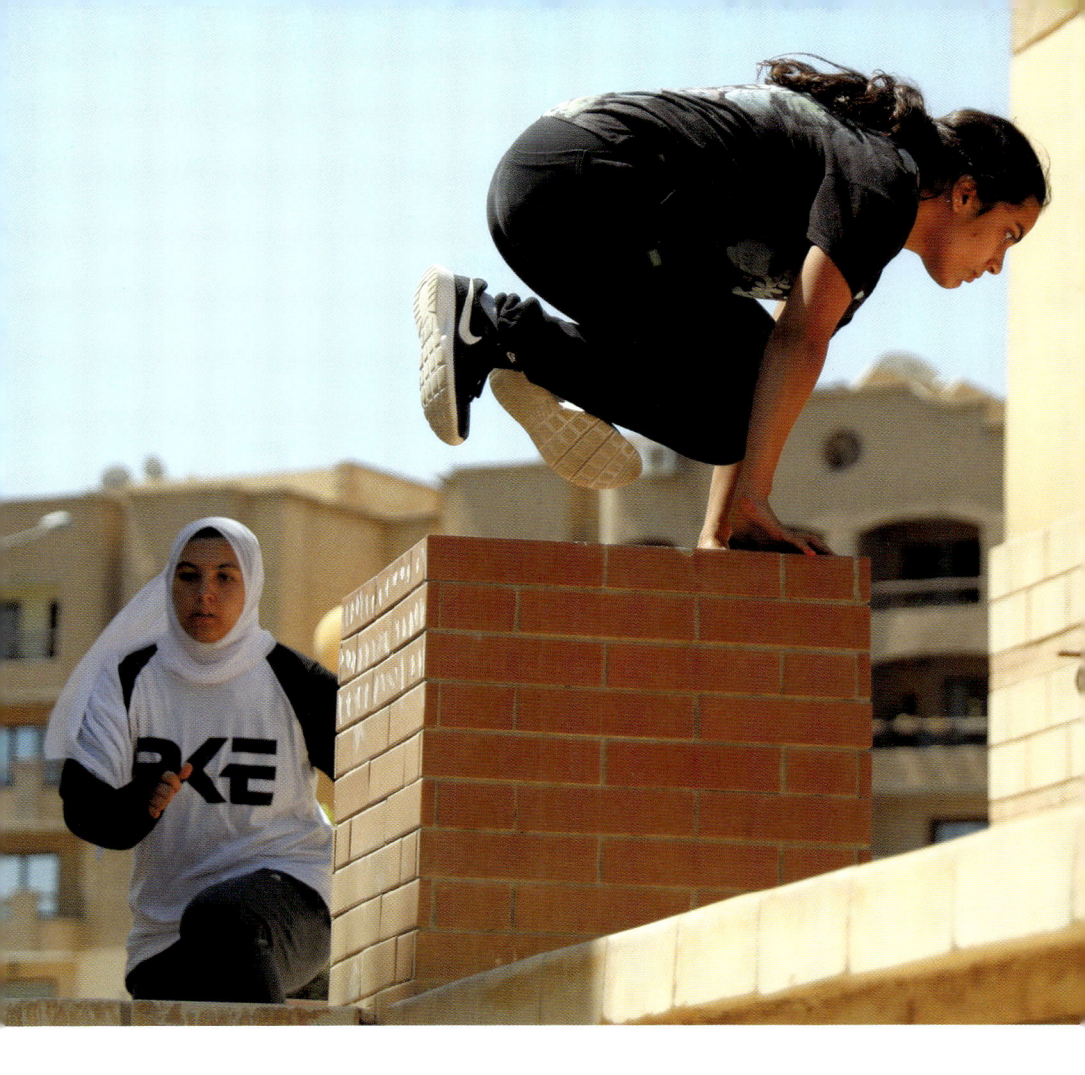

Two women practice parkour together in Egypt.

They prefer to focus on learning, training, and having fun.

Other traceurs go to competitions. In 2017, the International Gymnastics Federation (FIG) recognized parkour

An athlete runs through a parkour course in Greece.

as a sport. Since then, FIG has held competitions around the world. People come from all over to test their skills.

In a speed run, athletes look for the fastest way through an obstacle course.

Most competitions include speed runs and freestyle events. In a speed run, athletes go through a series of obstacles as fast as possible. The winner is the person with the fastest time.

In freestyle, athletes are judged on how they get past the obstacles. Judges watch their moves. They look for style, **efficiency**, and control.

> **DID YOU KNOW?**
> Most speed runs last between 15 to 30 seconds, depending on the course.

In freestyle, athletes perform fancier moves than they would in a speed run.

Each person moves through the course in his or her own way. But several moves are common. Traceurs often **vault** over obstacles. They use **underbars** to slide beneath railings. The **wall run** is another popular move. Traceurs always roll after jumping. This move helps protect their hands and feet.

PARKOUR MOVES

cat leap
leaping to grab the top of a wall in a crouch, then straightening the legs to launch up over the edge

precision jump
moving both arms and legs for balance when jumping between ledges or other small areas

roll
curling the body to protect the head, hitting the ground shoulders first, then untucking the feet to stand

tic-tac
bouncing off one obstacle to clear a second one

vault
placing the hands on an obstacle and swinging the legs over it

wall run
spiriting toward a wall and jumping feetfirst to take quick steps up it

SUPERSTAR
HIKARI IZUMI

- Hikari Izumi is a parkour athlete from Japan who competes around the world.

- She started to practice parkour when she was in high school.

- Izumi first saw parkour on a TV commercial. She decided she wanted to try it herself.

- Izumi had tried other sports. But she liked parkour because she could work at her own pace. She enjoyed being free to create her own movements.

Karla Castellanos Gonzalez (pictured) was one athlete Hikari Izumi competed against at the 2019 FIG World Cup.

- Izumi continued practicing parkour when she came to the United States for college in 2016. After graduating in 2018, she moved back to Japan.

- She placed first in the women's speed run at the 2019 FIG World Cup in Japan. She also won second place in freestyle.

CHAPTER 4
SAFETY

Safety has been a big concern since parkour started. **Traceurs** often risk dangerous falls. As a result, training is key. Training helps people know their limits. It also helps them build strength.

LEARN MORE HERE!

Experienced traceurs might jump off ledges or bounce off buildings.

Beginning traceurs use low obstacles, such as cement benches.

At first, traceurs practice low to the ground. They do small, easy moves. They repeat each move many times.

Gradually, they try harder courses and moves. With time and practice, traceurs can take on any obstacle.

Traceurs practice balancing during a workshop led by Laurent Piemontesi, one of the men who founded parkour.

DID YOU KNOW? Some companies make shoes specifically for parkour. The shoes are lightweight.

MAKING CONNECTIONS

TEXT-TO-SELF

Do you think parkour or freerunning sounds more fun? Why?

TEXT-TO-TEXT

Have you read books that describe how other athletes train? How does that training compare to training for parkour?

TEXT-TO-WORLD

In parkour, athletes often use their environment instead of special equipment. What extra challenges might this create?

GLOSSARY

efficiency – doing something with the least amount of work.

obstacle course – a path filled with objects (such as walls and fences) that a person must find a way to get past.

traceur – a person who practices parkour.

underbar – a move that involves grabbing a bar and swinging the body under it feetfirst.

vault – to jump over an obstacle by first placing the hands on it and then swinging the legs over.

wall run – a move that involves jumping at a wall feetfirst and taking quick steps up it to reach the top.

INDEX

Belle, David, 10–13, 15

competing, 16, 18–20, 24

Foucan, Sebastien, 15

freestyle, 20–21, 25

jump, 4, 6, 9, 13, 22–23

obstacle course, 8, 10, 12

speed run, 20–21, 25

training, 10, 17, 26

vault, 7, 22–23

wall run, 22–23

ONLINE RESOURCES
popbooksonline.com

Scan this code* and others like it while you read, or visit the website below to make this book pop!

popbooksonline.com/parkour

*Scanning QR codes requires a web-enabled smart device with a QR code reader app and a camera.